BY MY SIDE

Titles in Teen Reads:

Badger Publishing Limited, Oldmedow Road, Hardwick Industrial Estate, King's Lynn PE30 4JJ
Telephone: 01438 791037

www.badgerlearning.co.uk

BY MY SIDE

ANN EVANS

By My Side ISBN 978-1-78464-321-8

Publisher: Susan Ross
Senior Editor: Danny Pearson
Editorial Coordinator: Claire Morgan
Copyeditor: Cheryl Lanyon
Designer: Bigtop Design Ltd
Printed by Bell and Bain Ltd, Glasgow

2 4 6 8 10 9 7 5 3 1

CHAPTER 1

BLACKOUT

I see stars.

Flashing lights.

Blurred faces peering down at me.

I'm lying on the ground.

Maybe I'm lying in the road, or in the gutter. I could be on my bedroom floor. That wouldn't be so bad. Then I see that I'm indoors – four walls are spinning around me.

Slowly the spinning stops. Blurred faces come into focus. I'm on the classroom floor. Kids from my class are looking down at me – and Jake.

I groan and wish the floor would open up and swallow me.

"Lie still, Zoe. You've had another seizure," says my teacher, as if I didn't know.

Of course I've had another seizure I want to scream at her. *I'm not lying here for fun!*

And I don't want to lie still. I want to get up. I feel such a fool splat out on the floor. I bet my arms and legs have been jerking and twitching. Bet my tongue has been lolling out. Bet I've been dribbling.

I close my eyes, wanting to die.

"Move back! Give her some air," says Miss Howe. "Jake, get a chair."

"Yes, Miss!"

No, Jake! I want to shout. *Go away Jake. Don't look*

at me like this.

But I hear the scrape of a chair being placed close, and then Miss Howe is stroking my hair back from my face.

"Take your time, Zoe," she says, looking scared. She doesn't want me to drop dead in her class. That wouldn't be good for her CV would it?

"I'm OK," I tell her, trying to sit up.

They all shuffle back like they're scared of catching something. *You can't catch epilepsy!* I want to shout. *You're born with it.* Or, at least, I was. Born with some sort of messed-up brain. Lucky me!

Miss Howe and Emma help me to sit up. Then I get shakily to my feet. My head starts to spin now, legs go weak. Jake grabs me and stops me from hitting the floor again. He's strong.

They help me onto the chair. Emma and Miss Howe stay close. Their faces say how sorry they are for me.

Don't pity me! I want to scream.

"Back to your desks, everyone," says Miss Howe. She smiles at me – a pitying smile. "When you're ready, Zoe, we'll get you down to the office. We'll ring your mum to come and fetch you."

I nod, wishing I was home now, where no one stares and feels sorry for me. So I get up, trying not to wobble. Emma grabs me round the waist, and Jake hovers, looking like he's ready to catch me again.

I wish…

I wish he'd be this nice because he likes me. Not because he feels sorry for me.

But Jake is kind, so yeah, he's going to be nice to me – Zoe the loser!

He's more than nice, actually. He's gorgeous – really, really gorgeous! He's a bit taller than me, with crazy black hair and the cutest smile. He doesn't know I fancy him. He's never going to know that!

I walk slowly down the corridor, Emma on one side of me, Jake on the other.

"How are you feeling now, Zoe?" Emma asks, looking at me sadly.

"I'm OK," I say. But I'm not. My knee hurts, my shoulder hurts and my head hurts. I must have banged them all as I went down.

"You hit the floor with such a thud," says Emma.

"I saw you going," Jake says, looking at me with worried eyes. "I knew you were about to fit. You went so pale. I tried to catch you, only I wasn't quick enough. Sorry."

"I'm used to it," I shrug. "It's no big deal."

They sit me down on a chair in the office. Mrs Burns rings my mum. She doesn't even have to look up her number. She's done this so many times.

"Will you be all right?" Emma asks, looking like she can't wait to wash her hands of me and get back to her mates – her normal mates. Not ones who have seizures. Who twitch, eyes rolling, their body out of control, looking like they might drop dead any minute.

Who'd want a mate like that?

I totally understand why I don't get asked to their parties or the cinema. I'm too big a risk. Anyway, I don't want to go to their boring parties. And I can watch films at home. I wouldn't go out with them even if they did ask me.

"Your mum's on her way," says Mrs Burns. "Thank you, Emma and Jake. You can go back to your class now."

Jake gives me a sad little smile and, to my surprise, Emma hugs me. A big, warm hug.

"Take care," she says softly.

It's so stupid, but I feel my eyes starting to sting and fill up with tears. I choke them back. I mustn't cry. I'm a big enough loser as it is. I don't want them feeling even more sorry for me.

I'm glad when they go. I don't need their sympathy.

I don't need anyone.

CHAPTER 2

DON'T PITY ME

Mum and Dad don't make a fuss. It's all pretty normal to them. Zoe has a fit, someone rings them. I get picked up, taken home – or to hospital. It depends on how long I fit for and where it happens. Today it was four minutes, so I was told. Mum keeps a record. Four minutes is about normal for me.

Later, Mum's sitting at the table, reading a letter. She looks up at me. Her face is odd, like she's a bit excited, a bit nervous.

"I've applied for a dog for you," she says. "A very special dog..."

"What!" I yell. I hate dogs. I've still got the scar on my leg from a dog bite years ago.

"There's an organisation that trains dogs for people who suffer like you..."

I don't want to hear any more. "No!" I shout. "Isn't my life bad enough?"

"Zoe, listen..."

I don't want to listen. I run up to my room and slam the door. I can't believe my parents would do this to me. Now they want me to walk around with a special dog, so the whole world knows I'm not right in the head. Why don't they just hang a sign round my neck?

I stare into the mirror, hating what I see. No wonder no one wants to hang out with me. Spots and lank, mousy hair. Can't believe Jake caught me today. It's a wonder he could even stand touching me!

I try not to think about Jake. What's the point?

"Zoe!" Mum taps my door, comes in and sits on my bed. "They are called Seizure Alert Dogs. They are trained to know when you're about to have a seizure."

I point to my ankle and my scar. "Er... what about this?"

"You were four, and you were pulling the dog's ears."

"So it's my fault I got bitten?"

"No, Zoe. It was my fault. You were just little."

She puts her arm round me, like I'm still four. I shrug her off. But clearly she's not giving up.

"Anyway, these Seizure Alert Dogs. We go to the training centre, the staff get to know you and find a suitable dog..."

"Right! Well a spotty Dalmatian it is then!"

Mum groans. "Zoe, I do wish you would stop putting yourself down."

"Well, look at me!" I shout, pulling at my lank hair. "I'm hardly a supermodel, am I?"

She goes to stroke my hair. I shrug her off again.

She sighs. "You can go to the hairdresser's whenever you want, I keep telling you that."

"And if I have a seizure there?"

Why doesn't she understand? I don't want to go anywhere. I don't want people staring at me, pitying me. If I had my way I wouldn't even go to school.

"That's exactly why a Seizure Alert Dog will be good for you," Mum says, looking hopeful. "It warns you well before it happens. It gives you time to lie down safely."

"How does it know?" I snap. "Even I don't know."

"Well, we'll find out when we go," she says, heading for the door. "Friday morning. I've cleared it with school."

As soon as she's gone I slump down onto my bed. I didn't think my life could get any worse. But good old Mum has seen to that.

I dread school next day. All the kids hang out in groups and pairs. As I cross the playground they all stop chatting and look at me.

Lisa doesn't see me and keeps on talking about me. I know she's talking about me, as she's making her arms and legs jerk and her eyes roll.

Sue digs her in the ribs and nods my way. Lisa turns pink, then she giggles.

They link arms and walk away, whispering about me now.

Jake sees me and jogs over. "Hey! How you feeling?"

"Like you care!" I say, then wish I hadn't. His cute smile fades. He looks like I've just kicked him where it hurts.

"I do care, Zoe. We all do…"

"Look," I say glaring at him, "I don't need your pity! I don't need you feeling sorry for me."

Then Emma waves and skips over. "Zoe! You're looking so much better."

"Yes, that's because I'm not splat out fitting!" I tell her.

That shuts her up. But not for long. "Good! Anyway, I wanted to show you this fantastic new make-up. It covers spots and blemishes like magic."

I suddenly feel like my spots have erupted like molehills. I can see Jake's eyes flicking over my face. I want to die.

"It was buy-one-get-one-free," Emma goes on. "You can have this one, if you like."

"My sister uses that," Jake adds.

I feel stupid and ugly. I want to run away and hide. But, one by one, the kids in my class take turns in asking me how I am.

I hate the way they look at me.

And it's going to get worse.

Mum and her stupid idea about getting me a special dog!

And I bet it bites me.

CHAPTER 3

HONEY

Friday. Dog day!

I wear my jeans and ankle boots – to save me from dog bites. Dad drives. The Support Dog Centre is miles away, and I sit in the back of the car as the miles roll by.

I thought it would be like a hospital, but it's not. It's like a small village. There are rows of little flats and people walking dogs. I avoid them.

As we go into an office, Mum looks nervous. "Try to be open-minded, Zoe."

A woman called Lara greets us. No dog, thank goodness. We sit and talk.

"So have you ever had a pet dog, Zoe?"

"You've got to be joking!" I say.

Mum and Dad glare at me.

Lara yaks on. Stuff about the dog being well cared for. I listen, bored. I thought this was about my seizures not about dogs.

Finally, Lara heads to the door. "The dog I thought might be right for you, Zoe, is Honey. Like all our dogs, she's a rescue dog."

"Does she bite?"

"No," she says kindly. "She doesn't bite."

I get the feeling that Mum and Dad aren't too pleased with me. So I stare out the window until Lara comes back.

Minutes later, she comes in – with a dog. A big dog! My heart thuds. Mum and Dad make silly Aaah! sounds and fuss the dog. It ignores them and heads straight for me.

I shrink back, sweating. "Take it away!"

"Sit, Honey," Lara says softly.

The dog sits, but it's still too close. And it's staring! Big brown eyes set in long golden fur, fixed right on me.

"Why is it looking at me like that?"

"I think she likes you, Zoe," says Lara. "Would you like to stroke her?"

I shake my head. I'm starting to sweat with fear.

"Shall we all go for a walk then?" Lara suggests.

That sounds like a good idea. Anything is better than being stuck here. I don't move until Lara tells Honey to come. I see her swap glances with Mum and Dad. They look disappointed.

I feel like I've already failed the test.

We take a walk around the streets. Lara holds the lead, but Honey is right by my side. Her fur brushing my leg. After a while my heart starts to beat normally again.

"Would you like to hold Honey's lead?"

I'm about to say no, but Dad gives me a hopeful smile. "I'll give it a go."

It is so weird holding a dog's lead. She doesn't pull, and it's like she knows which way I want to go. I try to trick her, turning round suddenly, as if to go back. It surprises the adults, but not Honey.

The dog looks up at me. I swear there's a smile on her face.

"There's no fooling her!" I grin.

We walk on. Lara says how I'd have to stay here at the Centre for three weeks, training with Honey. That's if they decide I can have her.

There's a road ahead. There's no traffic, so I go to cross. But Honey stops. The lead jerks. I give it a tug. Honey doesn't move.

"What's wrong with her?" I ask.

"She won't let you cross until you tell her," says Lara. "She needs to know you're OK before stepping into the road."

"How clever!" I say looking down at Honey. "Come on, I'm OK – OK?" She seems to understand and walks on. Oddly, I'm smiling again.

Some people are coming our way. A trainer, a woman, a little girl and a small black dog. Normally, I'd cross the road if a dog was heading my way. But for some reason I don't feel scared.

Lara stops to fuss the dog and chat to the people.

The little girl pats Honey. "I like your dog. What's its name?"

"Honey, but she's not mine," I tell her, feeling a wave of sadness for the kid, knowing what her life is going to be like. "Is this your dog?"

"Yes. His name's Sooty."

Laura explains that he's a Seizure Assistance Dog – not quite the same as Honey.

"Sooty lets Jade's parents know if she's about to have a seizure."

I nod. "That's good."

The girl's mum looks at my parents. "Having Sooty has changed our lives. He's like Jade's guardian angel. I can sleep at night now. Sooty tells me if Jade is poorly."

We stand around chatting for a bit, then walk on.

"How do the dogs know?" I ask.

"They get to know you, and how you act," says Lara. "They pick up on changes in your behaviour. Things we aren't aware of ourselves."

Lara talks a lot. She's pretty good at answering our questions. By the time we get back to her office, I've got the hang of it. But still, the thought of having a dog by my side all the time would be so embarrassing.

I hate the way people stare at me now. It's going to be a hundred times worse. I don't want everyone to know I have seizures.

Lara goes off to get us tea and biscuits. Honey seems happy enough to lie down by my feet. Mum reaches down and strokes her.

"She's beautiful, isn't she?"

"Yes, but..."

Mum cuts in before I can say I don't want a dog. "And I'm so proud of you Zoe. You've put aside your fear of dogs. That's so brave of you!"

I am pleased with myself for that. It's not nice freaking out just because a dog is walking along the same bit of pavement as you.

Looking at this big, soft dog with long, golden fur and kind eyes makes me wonder what I was ever scared of. But when Honey suddenly sits up and stares at me again, I feel that familiar shiver of fear run down my spine.

"She's staring at me again, Mum."

"Well, she's getting to know you, dear."

"But I don't like her staring..."

Honey moves closer to me, her head on my knees now. Big eyes fixed on mine. My heart is starting to race. "Get her away, Dad."

Dad pulls on Honey's lead. "Here, girl. Here, Honey. Zoe doesn't need you to stare her out. Honey!"

Honey's gaze doesn't flicker. She starts pawing at my knee. I'm glad when Lara comes back with a tea tray.

Dad makes a joke of it. "Honey's getting a bit too close for comfort, I'm afraid."

With a frown, Lara quickly puts the tea tray down, and looks from Honey to me. "I think Honey is telling us that Zoe is about to have a seizure."

I almost scream. I want to run. I don't want to fit. And more than anything, I don't want to know it's about to happen.

"I'm not!" I cry, looking at Mum and Dad. They're on their feet, panicking. They aren't used to knowing about it beforehand either.

Lara strokes Honey, tells her what a good girl she is. Gives her a treat. "I'm amazed she's picked up on you so soon, Zoe."

"She's wrong!" I argue. "She's just a dog. She can't know."

Lara just smiles. "Let's get you into one of our flats and get you comfy."

I'm led out of the office and into the flat next door. Mum and Dad hold onto me like I'm about to drop dead at any second. The dog walks beside me, tail wagging.

Then I get it! Honey knows she gets a treat if she taps a person's knee. Crafty dog!

But she seems to have fooled Lara. Lara puts cushions and pillows on the floor. Making a comfy, safe place for me to lie down in.

I humour them. "I'm not going to fit, Mum. Honey was just after a doggy treat."

Lara nods. "It is unusual for a dog and the person to bond so quickly. But to be on the safe side, I'd like you to lie down, Zoe."

I lie down, surrounded by cushions. I smile up at Mum and Dad. I even reach out and stroke Honey's fur. It's so soft. She whines, and puts her paw in my hand.

And that's the last thing I know.

CHAPTER 4

JUST A DOG

Monday morning and I'm walking into school – dog-less. It's weird, but since meeting Honey, then leaving her at the Centre, I've had an odd feeling inside. A sort of empty feeling. It's not nice.

I spot Jake by the school gates, just hanging about, like he's waiting for someone.

I keep my head down as I go past him.

"Zoe! Hey! How was the dog place?"

"Er, well it works," I say, surprised when he falls

into step with me. He couldn't have been waiting for me, could he?

"How d'ya mean?"

"The dog warned me I was going to have a seizure and guess what? I did!"

"That's good, isn't it?"

I shrug. "You tell me."

"I'd say so. You get the chance to prepare yourself, so you don't just fall on the ground and hurt yourself." His voice trailed away. "I hate it when that happens to you..."

I glance at him, but he's looking away.

"Me and dogs don't get on," I tell him. "Anyway..."

I stop. I was about to tell him that I hate being stared at. That a Seizure Alert Dog would only make people stare at me all the more.

But it's too embarrassing to tell Jake that. He'd only feel even more sorry for me.

Then he smiles and looks at me with those gorgeous brown eyes. "I love dogs. I've got a little Staffi called Bob. Hey, if you do get a dog, we could walk them in the park."

Like that was going to happen!

He was just being kind. He probably wouldn't want to be seen dead with me.

*

The days go by, and I'm doing my best not to think of Honey. It's stupid but I can't help it. I guess she's been put with someone else by now. Better for her. I'm no good with dogs.

Emma keeps asking if I've got any news. I tell her I'm not bothered.

By Friday I'm really not bothered.

It would be too embarrassing.

But on Friday after school, there's a visitor –
Lara. I feel excited for a second. But there's no
sign of the dog and the feeling dies.

Mum and Dad are giving me that look! The one
that says, *please don't say the wrong thing.*

Lara smiles. "Hello, Zoe. How are you?"

What she really means is have I had a
seizure today.

"OK, thanks," I answer, sitting down by Mum.

I soon see why she's here. And why Mum and
Dad are looking so tense. I'm to have Honey. My
very own Seizure Alert Dog. I don't know if
I should laugh or cry.

So I do nothing.

They carry on telling me what will happen now.
Me and Mum will go to the Centre and live there

for three weeks. Me and Honey will get to know each other and I'll learn how to take care of her.

I listen and nod in all the right places. I even smile and try to look happy. By the time Lara goes, I'm feeling a bit shell-shocked.

Mum and Dad are over the moon.

"It's wonderful news!" Mum gushes, giving me a quick hug.

Dad plants a kiss on the top of my head. "It will make such a difference to us all."

I don't see why. It's just a dog.

*

At the Centre, I swear Honey smiled when she saw me again. And it wasn't just her tail that wagged, it was her whole back end!

Mum and me were staying in one of the little flats. The trainer was a tall guy who had made it his job to make me smile. By the end of the three weeks it had worked.

I was a bit sad to leave. I liked it there. No one stared. No one felt sorry for me.

But Honey and me were all trained up and ready for the big, bad world.

I'd had four seizures over the three weeks. Mum and Lara had been with me once. Mum and my trainer the other times. Honey had given me a ten-minute warning each time.

I have to say, she is one smart dog.

*

Back home, Honey's bed is in my bedroom. She seems OK. We're all OK. But Monday morning comes and I'm all jittery.

"Do you want me to come to school with you, Zoe?" Mum asks.

"No, I'll be fine," I say, as I put Honey into her coat. The one that will tell the world I've got brain problems. I've made up my mind. If the kids want to laugh and stare and take the Mickey, let them.

Mum waves me goodbye. Like I'm off on a big adventure.

In a way, I am.

A few people look as we walk down the street. I try not to let it bother me. But near school, there are crowds of kids. They stop and gape.

I feel shaky.

I hate this. I feel so stupid.

At school, they step aside for me and Honey. They all stare. My face is burning. Then Sue and Lisa rush over. Big smiles on their faces.

"Oh! He's beautiful!" Lisa says, crouching down next to Honey.

"He's a she," I tell her.

Lisa looks up. "She's adorable. What's her name?"

"Honey."

"Is it OK to stroke her?" asks Sue.

Honey's tail is wagging, but she stays close by my leg. "Yes, I think she likes it."

They both pat and stroke Honey. Then more kids come over. But it's not me they're looking at. It's my dog. And a million questions come my way.

By the time we get into class, I realise I've talked more in that ten minutes than I do in a week!

Emma gives me a hug when she sees me. "I'm so happy for you," she says.

I can't believe it. There are tears in her eyes.

Class starts and, with all the fuss, I hadn't seen Jake. I spot him now, at his desk. He looks at me, then looks away.

My heart drops into my shoes.

I knew it. He wouldn't be seen dead with me now.

I don't care! I tell myself. *I don't care!*

CHAPTER 5

ALONE

At break and lunch time, lots of kids hang around. I have to tell them not to feed Honey scraps of food. The day flies by. It's been a good day. Except for Jake not speaking to me.

I look around for him. He's gone.

More kids want to pet Honey and ask me questions. So I'm late getting out of school. I don't mind. I can't believe how good today has been. Then my heart leaps.

Jake is by the school gates!

"That's Jake," I say softly to Honey. Over the last few weeks, I've told Honey a lot about Jake. In fact, I've told her a lot about me and how I feel. Well, she's not going to tell anyone, is she? My secrets are safe with her.

"Hi," Jake says.

"Hi." I keep walking. He falls into step beside me. I wish my heart would stop racing.

"So, this is Honey. Can I say hello?"

I stop. Jake bends down and takes Honey's head in his hands. "Hello, Honey. I'm Jake."

I want to giggle. "She'll shake hands with you, if you want."

He looks up with those gorgeous brown eyes. Then looks back at my dog. He holds out his hand. "Pleased to meet you, Honey."

She raises her paw.

Jake says, "Now, you have a very important job to do, Honey. You have to take good care of my friend, Zoe. OK?"

My eyes sting.

I can't hide the tears as he stands up and looks right into my eyes. He doesn't say a word. He just puts his arms around me and holds me close.

Honey makes a bored little noise and sits down.

Jake walks me back home. We chat about all sorts. I even have the nerve to ask him in. Mum gives him a slice of her home-made cake and asks him to stay for dinner.

To my amazement, he says yes.

Later in the week, I meet his Staffi, Bob. The two dogs have a great time at the park.

The kids at school are getting used to Honey now. We're like a double-act. It's *Hi Honey, Hi Zoe!* She's the star, and I've never been happier.

I'm getting my hair styled on Friday, and going to see a film with a few kids from my class on Saturday – and yes, Jake's coming too!

Mum and Dad have gone out tonight. Theatre, then a meal. I can't remember the last time they had a night out together. But they know I'm OK with Honey by my side. I put a film on, tuck my feet under me and relax. Honey is flat out on the rug, asleep.

After a while she wakes up and pads over to me.

"Need a wee?" I get up, and head to the door. But she gets in front of me. Stopping me. Looking at me. "I can't let you out unless you move, Honey."

She doesn't move.

She stays. Looking up at me. Staring at me.

"What?"

She starts to paw my leg.

I go icy cold.

For a minute my mind goes blank. Then panic sets in. I try to think what to do. Find a safe place. Lie down. Ring for help. But my legs refuse to move.

Honey shuffles closer, pushes me with her nose. Makes me move.

I jump into action.

I drag the cushions off the sofa and chairs, make a nest for myself on the floor. I ring Mum. And get the answer phone.

"Think I'm about to fit. Time is five to eight." I hang up.

Honey stays close.

My film is still on. "We were just getting to the good bit," I say. My weak attempt at a joke.

Honey paws my leg again. Whines. She's telling me to lie down. So I lie down.

And wait.

How weird, lying on the floor, waiting. I wish Mum and Dad were here. I'm scared. I'd rather not know. But at least I'm not going to hit my head on anything sharp or hard. I'm already on the floor. Well padded for when my arms and legs start to thrash about.

My heart is thudding.

Then Honey lies down with me. Her head by mine. She moves closer, puts her paws over my chest. Like she's holding me. Keeping me safe.

"Good girl," I say. Then lie still – and wait.

*

The room is spinning. A blur of gold streaks, round and round. It slows. Comes into focus. Honey. Her breath is warm on my face. She licks me. A big, slobbery lick. Like she's saying wake up!

I lie still for a while. Then slowly sit up. Honey stays close, letting me lean on her. The film is still on. I don't seem to have missed much. The cushions are in a mess.

When I can stand, I put them back on the chairs. Flop back down.

Honey wags her tail and I give her a treat.

Mum and Dad arrive in a mad panic.

"Zoe, I'm so sorry we weren't here for you," Mum frets. "Poor you, going through it all by yourself. All alone!"

I tell them both not to panic. It's all fine. I'm fine.

"And I wasn't alone, Mum... I'm not alone." I wrap my arms around Honey. Press my face into her fur. "I have Honey by my side now."

THE END